BLOOD
ON TAP

BLOOD ON TAP

Edgar J. Hyde

© 1998 Children's Choice Publications Ltd

Text supplied by Alan J. Henderson

ISBN 1-902012-12-7

Printed and bound in the UK

Contents

Chapter 1

It was time for dinner. The six of us sat squeezed around the table in the cramped little kitchen. Mum and Dad sat at either end of the table. My younger brother, Gary, sat beside me. I'm Alex, by the way, Alex Todd. Opposite us sat my two younger sisters Beth and Karen. Our elbows clashed as we tried to eat our food.

"This is ridiculous," said Dad.

Mum agreed and said, "I know we'll need to get a bigger place soon."

When we moved into this house eight years ago it seemed big enough for us. Since then we've had additions to the family in the shapes of Karen and Gary. Karen was now four and Gary was eight years old. Beth was eleven going on twelve and was, by two years, my junior.

With only three small bedrooms, a living room and a small kitchen, it was obvious that we had outgrown the house.

"I think we've saved enough to make the move soon," said Dad.

Mum quizzed him.

"But we've saved barely a few thousand pounds. How will we get a bigger place with that amount of money?"

"Ah!" said Dad with one of his knowing smiles.

We all knew and recognised what that smile meant. It must be one of Dad's great ideas. Dad was famous for these. Every one of them usually turned into a disaster. Strangely, it never put Dad off coming up with them from time to time. I suppose they kept us entertained at least.

Dad continued, "I heard about this huge house a few miles from here. Dick in the office told me about it. He said it was going at a reasonable price for its size."

"You mean cheap?" said Mum with a knowing look at Dad.

Dad shrugged his shoulders.

"Dick said it may need some work done on it, but I'm sure we'll be able to handle that."

"Oh, you think so, do you?" said Mum with a stern look towards Dad.

"Well, it would be better than being stuck in here like sardines in a tin," Dad reasoned.

We looked at each other and nodded in agreement. The house was just too small. Something had to be done about it. If that meant moving to a new area, going to new schools and making new friends then it had to be.

"At least let's all go and see it," said Dad.

Mum sighed.

"I suppose it won't do any harm to look," she said unconvincingly. "What do you kids think?"

I cried, "I'm all for it. I want a room of my own."

Beth agreed and said, looking towards her younger brother and sister, "Yes, it would be nice to get some privacy around here."

"Will it have more than one bathroom?" asked Gary. "I hate queuing for the toilet in the morning."

"I expect so, but we'll just have to wait and see," replied Dad.

Mum turned to Karen, our youngest family member.

"What about you Karen? Have you got anything to say?"

Karen thought for a while before she spoke. It was one of her little traits. You could ask her the simplest of questions and wait ages for an answer. Sometimes it drove me mad.

Then she spoke, "As long as it's not spooky. I hate ghosts."

We all laughed and Dad said, "Don't worry little one. Ghosts only exist in stories. If there are any, Dad will frighten them away."

"Who's the agent selling the place?" Mum asked Dad.

"It's a private sale to be arranged through a Miss Davina Metz," said Dad.

"Sounds foreign; never heard of her," said Mum with disapproval.

Dad rose to his feet and said, "I'll give her a call right away. We don't want to miss out on the opportunity of a lifetime, do we?"

Beth and Karen squeezed in towards the

table to allow Dad to pass. Dad, being Dad though, still managed to trip on a chair leg and stumbled out of the room. I could barely stifle a laugh at the clumsiness of my Dad. Mum looked at me, trying to hide a smile as well.

From the kitchen we heard Dad on the phone in the hallway.

"Hello. Davina Metz? This is Bill Todd. I'm interested in the big property out of town," he said.

"Yes – Yes – That would be fine – great! See you then," he concluded and hung up the phone.

Dad bounced back into the kitchen rubbing his hands with glee.

"Well?" asked Mum.

Dad answered, "We can all go and see the place tomorrow evening."

My brothers and sisters looked at each other in disbelief. Dad had done it again. Of all the evenings to visit a house – Wednesday was the busiest for all of us. I had football practice, Beth went horse riding and Gary had swimming lessons on that particular night of the week. Even, Karen, who was only four, usually went to see Granny with Mum on a Wednesday.

I was the first to object and said, "If I miss football practice I might not get in the team."

Dad joked, "You're so good you don't need to practise."

If only that were true, I thought to myself.

"Sammy will miss me, Dad, if I'm not there tomorrow," Beth added.

"There's plenty of other kids to feed him sweets," he replied to Beth.

"If I don't learn to swim I might drown," said Gary joining in.

Dad smiled.

"I'll always be there to save you Gary," he said.

Mum and Karen were not impressed with Dad's arrangement at all.

"You know how much she enjoys seeing Granny," said Mum.

Dad held his hands up in a gesture of surrender, sighed.

"Yes, yes, OK. I know I chose the wrong evening to see the house. But I just want what's best for all of us – and that's a bigger house. It could be a great place to live and we would kick ourselves if we missed the chance to see it and put in an offer for it."

Dad's plea made sense to us all. Although he had chosen the worst possible evening to visit the house, he was only trying to do the best for us. Dad was always that way. He was often clumsy and appeared stupid sometimes, but he always had our best interests at heart.

Beth then added,

That night we all went to bed with the exciting thought of going to see a house where we might end up living. It could be the start of a new life for us all.

Chapter 2

At six o'clock on the Wednesday evening we bundled into the car. The house was only a few miles away and would take us about fifteen minutes to reach. This was usually more than enough time for all us kids to end up fighting with each other. Car journeys involving the whole family were always fraught affairs.

"Best behaviour now kids!" said Mum.

We drew each other long looks as Mum spoke. I wondered who would be the first to spark off trouble this time?

After a few minutes I asked Dad, "What's the name of the part of town where the house is?"

"Oddburgh," replied Dad.

"What? Odd . . . Burgh?" I said in disbelief.

"I know it's a bit of a strange name but we'll get used to it," Dad answered.

"I've never been over to that part of town," said Mum.

"Me neither," agreed Dad.

If Mum and Dad had never been in Oddburgh before, then it was certain us kids had not been there either.

"It's a quiet part of town, so I'm told," said Dad.

Mum continued, "Marion, next door, said there's a lot of money in Oddburgh. The schools are better too."

"Maybe thick Gary will stand a better chance then!" cried Beth.

It had started. World War III in the back seat of the car was about to commence. The only surprise was it had taken more than five minutes to begin.

Gary cried back at her, "Shut up swot!"

"Kids! Behave!" shouted Mum.

Gary stuck his tongue out at Beth, but she ignored him and held her head high in the air. She often ignored Gary's presence in this way and it annoyed him even more. Fortunately, we were nearing our destination.

Dad turned the car into a tree-lined road called Blackday Avenue.

"Nice name!" I quipped.

Dad explained, "It was named after a local businessman, Arthur Blackday."

"It should be up here somewhere on the left," said Dad.

As we went further up the road, the trees seemed to close in on us and it became quite dark. I could see my brother and sisters were quite spooked by the sudden loss of light. Who would want to live in such a gloomy area?

"These trees sure need pruned," said Mum.

Dad joked, "There's a job for you Alex!"

I groaned as Dad said this. He was always wanting me to do odd jobs around the garden to earn my pocket money.

"Don't tease the boy," said Mum.

The car stopped suddenly outside a gateway.

"This must be the place," cried Dad.

We passed between two huge iron gates and up a long tree lined driveway.

I felt uneasy as I looked at the number on the gates. It was number 13!

"More pruning needed here, Alex!" cried Dad as he laughed to himself.

Nobody else in the car was laughing though. There the house loomed in front of us in the dim light. It was massive. Far bigger than any of us had really imagined.

We clambered out of the car to have a better view of it. Built from a dark stone and with several turrets it looked very imposing – almost like a castle. What I mean is that it really looked scary!

"Funny, the Estate Agent's car isn't here?" noted Dad.

Mum said, "Maybe she's late?"

"I'll try the door anyway," said Dad.

We walked up to a gigantic black door that had gargoyles above it on either side. Their devilish faces looked down upon us. Who would want to live here and be greeted by those ugly faces each time they arrived home?

Father pushed the bell and we waited.

"Looks fantastic doesn't it?" beamed Dad.

I couldn't believe it. He really seemed to like the place!

Mum replied with little enthusiasm, "It certainly looks big enough for us."

We waited and waited but nobody came to answer the door.

"Maybe she got the dates mixed up?" explained Dad.

Mum laughed and said, "Could it be maybe YOU got the dates mixed up!"

"No way!" replied Dad with a hint of hurt in his voice.

He seemed really quite upset that he was not going to see his wonderful house. The rest of us were not upset to get away from the place though. I could sense that the others already felt the same way about the place as me. It gave us the creeps!

We turned away from the door and began walking back to the car.

Suddenly there was the loudest and creakiest door opening I've ever heard. We were all frozen to the spot as it happened.

A croaky voice then said, "Good evening Mr Todd."

I turned around to see a tall slim figure in the dimly lit doorway.

"Ah! You must be Davina Metz," cried Dad.

She was a woman I reckoned was in her thirties, although it was hard to tell. Dressed from head to toe in black and with ivory white skin and long black hair, she looked a frightening sight. She was exactly like a character you would expect to see in a horror movie.

"Please do come in," she said.

We looked at each other knowing that we really didn't want to enter the house with our strange and eerie looking guide. We had no other choice though.

Dad ushered us forward.

"Come on! What's up with you lot?"

The floorboards creaked as we stepped

into a large dark hallway. The place smelled old and unused. That sort of damp musty smell with an added hint of moth-balls.

Miss Metz said, "I apologise for the lack of light. A fuse must have blown some-where. We'll have to view the property by candlelight I'm afraid."

"That's OK. I'm sure it will give the house a romantic feel," said Dad.

Mum groaned as he said that. How could he actually like the place already?

Miss Metz pointed upstairs with a long white boney finger and said, "We'll begin at the top."

"Anything you say," said Dad full of en-thusiasm.

We climbed a long creaky staircase lit only with candles dotted here and there. On the walls were wild animal trophies of bear and deer heads.

Karen looked at them and whispered to me, "Are those real, Alex?"

"Yes, I think so," I replied.

Karen continued, "Where are their bodies then?"

This was typical of Karen. She was only four and didn't understand about hunting and trophies.

"It doesn't matter?" I briskly replied

Coming to a halt on the landing, Miss Metz pointed to the attic hatch.

"I'd pull down the ladder and show you the attic but there's very little to see in this poor light," she explained.

I could see that Mum wanted to have a look anyway, but Dad jumped in front of her and said, "That's OK. Just show us the rest of the house."

There were six bedrooms and a bathroom upstairs. The bathroom looked ancient with huge brass taps. It was very large though. In fact, the bathroom was larger than any of our bedrooms in our present house.

Mum whispered to Dad, "This wouldn't look out of place in a museum."

"Yes its got real character hasn't it!" replied Dad.

I still couldn't believe what I was hearing. He seemed to be in love with the creepy place.

Moving downstairs we were shown through four large living rooms, a vast kitchen, again with ancient plumbing and another bathroom. Arriving back in the hallway Miss Metz stood in front of a door situated under the staircase.

"This leads to the basement she announced," she announced.

Dad asked her, "Is it huge as well?"

"Yes it is quite big. However, as we have no electricity, I think it's too dangerous to go down there at the moment," she stated.

Dad nodded in agreement and said, "Quite right."

"I'll leave you to look around," said our guide as she turned and disappeared into the kitchen.

Excited, Dad asked, "What do you think of it kids?"

We looked at each other wondering what to say to Dad. It was obvious he was in love with the house and none of us wanted to hurt his feelings.

Beth began, "It's certainly big enough."

"See, I told you so. All the space in the world!" he cried.

Trying to be diplomatic I said, "It's a bit old. Wouldn't we be better off in a more modern place?"

"Yes, at twice the price!" cried Dad.

I could tell I had upset him. He really did seem to see something in the place that none of the rest of us could. Mum stood there with a forlorn look on her face.

"What about you, Honey?" he asked Mum.

Mum sighed and replied, "It's going to need so much work done to it."

"I can do some of it," said Dad.

"Plumbing and the electric too?" questioned Mum.

Dad shrugged his shoulders and said, "Maybe not those jobs. But I've got loads of contacts to get the tradesmen to do that sort of stuff."

Mum shook her head and said, "I just don't know. It's so dark and gloomy. I'm not sure if I could ever get to like a place such as this."

Dad sounding upbeat said, "Wait until you see it in daylight and when the power is back on. I'm sure you'll change your mind about it then."

My sisters and brother were looking at me with quizzical expressions on their faces, which suggested they thought Dad was a bit loopy. How could he possibly hope to persuade a person as sensible as Mum into coming to live in a creepy old place like this?

He turned to us and said, "You lot will love it too when you see it under better lighting."

We could offer no response to his obvious enthusiasm for the house.

"Right then! I'll go and find this Davina Metz to tell her we could be interested" cried Dad as he strode off to find the strange Estate Agent.

As Dad went off in the direction that Miss Metz was last seen, Mum turned to me.

"Your father has a real feeling about this house you know," she said.

"I can see that. Is he really serious?" I inquired.

Mum sighed and said, "Well kids, it is going for a very attractive price."

"You mean dirt cheap," said Beth.

Mum smiled and said, "If you want to put it that way, yes!"

Karen then said, "But it's so spooky Mum. Dad wouldn't make us live here, would he?"

Seeing that my little sister Karen was upset at even the thought of us moving here, Mum reassured her.

"The place isn't haunted Karen. There's no such thing as ghosts."

"I thought that Davina Metz was a ghost when I first saw her at the door," said Gary.

Mum scolded Gary, "Keep your voice down! She might have heard that comment."

Reappearing after a minute Dad said, "I can't find her anywhere. She didn't go upstairs did she?"

"No, we haven't seen her," I replied.

Dad scratched his head and said, "I'll just have a look around upstairs anyway."

Mum cautioned him, "Be careful the house is only dimly lit and you might trip."

"Of course I'll be careful," said Dad.

As he set off up the stairs he did exactly what we all thought he would do. He tripped up the first step. We tried not to giggle. It was so typical of our Dad.

"Are you all right?" asked Mum.

Dad didn't reply and went up the stairs to look for the elusive Miss Metz. To where had the strange woman disappeared?

He came back down a few seconds later and said, "I can't find her anywhere. How odd."

"We can't hang around here all night waiting for her," said Mum.

Dad nodded his head and said, "I'll try calling her. Hello! Miss Metz!"

After waiting a few seconds he called again, "Miss Metz we'd like to speak to you now!"

Still there was no reply. Where could she have disappeared?

"I hope she's not fallen down the stairs to the basement," said Gary trying to be funny.

Dad frowned and said, "Don't be funny, Gary. She didn't go near that door, did she?"

"No, she definitely headed towards the kitchen when she left us," I replied to Dad.

With a puzzled look upon his face Dad said, "Maybe she got called away or something. You know what these people are like with their mobile phones."

Mum nodded and said, "We'll just have to close the door behind us as we leave."

We walked back out into the evening air and Dad closed the door behind us. It shut with a long creaking sound and a loud thud.

It felt good to outside again. Dad had a last look around for Miss Metz but to no avail. She had simply vanished.

Driving back home in the car, Dad was in a happy mood. We could always tell he was happy because of his dreadful whistling. He actually liked the house.

Chapter 3

That evening as I lay in bed I could hear Mum and Dad talking about the house. They talked for hours and hours. Sometimes their voices were raised and sometimes they were laughing. Surely Dad couldn't convince Mum that this was the house for us!

I fell asleep and awoke early the next morning. After washing and dressing I went downstairs to have some breakfast. Only Mum and Dad were up. They looked as if they hadn't slept very much last night.

"Usual for breakfast, Alex?" Mum asked me.

"Yes, thanks Mum," I replied.

Dad then arose from the breakfast table and strode towards the phone saying, "I'm going to call that Davina Metz woman."

"It's a bit early isn't it?" said Mum.

Dad had the phone in his hand and said, "She did say I could call her at this number night or day."

Dad punched the number and waited a few seconds.

"Hello, Miss Metz? It's Bill Todd here. The family that came to see the house last night," explained Dad.

He continued, "We seemed to miss each other last night and I just wanted to register an interest in the property."

Miss Metz must have then spoken for quite a while because Dad didn't say a word for a few minutes.

"OK we're definitely interested. I'll be in touch," confirmed Dad.

He put down the phone and clapped his hands in joy. Mum looked towards the floor as I looked at her for an explanation of what was going on. Surely she hadn't ended up agreeing with him?

Mum said, "I'm sorry I couldn't tell you first, but your father and me have decided to try and buy that house."

My jaw dropped. I couldn't believe what she had said. How could she possibly want to move to that house? It would be a ghastly place to live.

"But it's a horrible old place!" I cried.

Dad responded, "It's not that bad. With a lick of paint it will be fine. You'll love it."

Mum added, "Alex, it's big enough for all of us and it's in a good area with good schools. It's also in our price range."

"Can't we try to see other places?" I pleaded.

"For the price Miss Metz is asking it won't

be on the market for long. We've got to act quickly on this one or we'll regret it" explained Dad.

How had he done it? What could Dad have said to convince Mum that moving to that old monstrosity was a good idea? I mean, our Dad is well known for being a bit daft, but Mum was supposed to be so sensible. Had she finally cracked as well?

I was not very happy with Mum but, resigned myself to the fact that we might be moving, I said, "Maybe it's not so bad after all."

"That's the spirit, Alex," said Dad.

One by one the rest of the family came down to breakfast and the news about our possible move. Each time as it was explained their jaws dropped just like mine had. That was except for Karen, who immediately burst into tears.

She screamed, "Not there! It's a spooky

horrible place with ghosts and nasty things!'

Cuddling her, Mum reassured her.

"There are no ghosts in that house. If by any chance there are, then Dad will chase them away forever."

"Yes, just watch me!" cried Dad bending his arms to flex his biceps.

We all laughed at his silly show of strength.

Beth asked Mum, "What convinced you that trying to buy that old place was a good idea? We didn't really get a good look at the place and that woman was just plain weird."

Mum sighed and replied, "We've got to move soon, otherwise this house will burst at the seams. It's a bigger house and the price is very attractive."

Looking unconvinced Beth said, "Are you sure?"

"Well, your Dad assures me everything will turn out alright this time," Mum added.

Beth raised her eyebrows in disbelief and said, "We'll see about that?"

Dad whom, as usual, hadn't been paying any attention to the conversation around him suddenly cried:

"I'm glad we're all agreed that it's a good idea to move. I'll phone the bank and the lawyer as soon as they open for business."

With that, Dad left the room whistling a merry tune without a care in the world. He seemed so happy with himself. I shook my head and thought he must be mad. What seemed worse was that Mum no longer seemed totally sane either.

Chapter 4

Later that afternoon the phone rang. As usual, there was an almighty race between Gary, Beth and myself to see who could be the first to answer it. Whoever had control of the phone was king in our household. Gary seemed the favourite to answer it, but a last minute slip on the rug allowed me to breeze past him and pick up the receiver. I grinned with delight at my victory as I answered the phone.

"Is that you Alex?" said Dad.

"Yes, what can I do for you?" I replied.

"Great news!" Dad cried, "I've spoken to the bank manager and the lawyer and we're going to put in an offer for the house today."

I was lost for words. How could things happen so quickly?

"Alex, are you still there?" queried Dad. "Isn't that great news?"

Trying to sound enthusiastic I replied, "Wonderful Dad, just wonderful."

"Is your Mum there? I want to tell her the fantastic news," said Dad.

I shouted to Mum, "It's Dad on the phone."

She rushed to the phone to hear the awful news that Dad had told to me. It could have been worse though. Dad could have phoned to say that his offer to buy the house had been accepted. That would have been a shocker!

Rounding up my brother and sisters I told them the terrible news.

Chapter 4

"Dad has put in an offer for that place," I stated to them.

"Oh no! How could he?" said Beth.

"I don't know. He just seems in love with that spooky old house," I answered.

"Maybe we should have objected more to his plans," said Gary.

I shrugged my shoulders and said, "I don't think it would have made much difference. You know what he's like when he's got an idea in his head."

Karen, surprisingly, spoke very clearly and calmly.

"We'll have to change his mind for him then!"

It was not like Karen to be this sure about anything. She was only four after all.

"What do you mean by that?" I questioned her.

She produced an impish smile across tiny face.

"We'll spook him out of the place," she said.

We all laughed at her idea. Here was a four-year-old proposing to scare our Dad out of his dream home. It would never work. Or would it? One by one, Beth, Gary and myself began to realise the potential of Karen's plan. Dad was exactly the sort of person who might easily be spooked!

Eventually, at 5 o'clock, the phone rang again. We all guessed who it was and what he was about to tell us. For the first time in ages there was no great rush to answer the phone. It rang and rang as my brother and sisters looked at each other not wanting to get to their feet and answer the phone.

Mum yelled, "Will somebody answer that phone, I'm busy!"

As I was the oldest I decided that I had better do it.

I lifted the receiver, took a deep breath

and without waiting to hear Dad speak I said: "The house is ours Dad?"

"Yes it is, Alex! How did you know it was me, and how did you know what I was going to tell you?" said Dad.

"Oh, just a wild guess," I replied.

"It's fantastic!" Dad continued. We can move in as soon as possible once our own place is sold. Can you tell Mum the great news? I've got to go now."

Putting down the receiver, I turned to Beth, Gary and Karen. They knew from my forlorn expression what my news was to be.

"We've got the house," I groaned to them.

Beth nodded her head.

"OK, we'll have to think of ways to spook Dad out of there then," she said.

"Mum!' I shouted. "That was Dad. The offer's been accepted and we can move as soon as our place is sold."

Mum entered the room and gave us all a

big hug. She understood that we were not really pleased at the idea of moving to that old place.

"It's for the best kids. I'm sure you'll grow to like the house as much as your Dad does," said Mum.

Over the next few days many people came to view our house. It was our last hope that nobody would want to buy it. If Dad couldn't sell our current home, then he couldn't afford to buy the spooky old place. Despite being told to keep the house tidy and to be polite to all the visitors we tried our best to put them off buying the property.

We tried leaving toys and comics everywhere to make the house look like a dump. This failed miserably. Anybody who looked at our finely constructed mess just smiled and said: "Kids!"

Even though we knew we should never

be rude, we stuck our tongues out at viewers and picked our noses. Although we tried staring and pointing at people to put them off buying our house our, it didn't work.

After only a few days on the market Dad received numerous offers. He was beaming with delight. The move was progressing along very smoothly for him.

With a huge grin, Dad announced to Mum, "We've made a far better price than I ever thought we would."

Mum smiled back and stated, "For once you may have got things right!"

They kissed.

"Hey kids! We'll be moving at the end of next week," announced Dad.

We didn't know what to say. Mum and dad looked so happy with themselves that we didn't want to upset their moment of enjoyment.

Karen cried, "Great! I can't wait to move."

We knew that what she really meant was she couldn't wait to start scaring Dad into changing his mind about the creepy old house.

Chapter 5

As our new home needed a lot of work done to it, Dad began to phone around his contacts over the next few days. When we had visited the place it obviously needed new plumbing, wiring and a lot of work done to the gardens.

Dad had phoned an electrician by the name of Mr Kruger and invited him around to talk about what needed done to our new home. He arrived the following day.

"Where exactly is your new place, Mr Todd?" inquired Mr Kruger.

Dad answered, "It's in Oddburgh. A street called Blackday Avenue."

Mr Kruger's face turned white as my dad spoke. What was wrong with him?

"Not number 13, is it?" inquired Mr Kruger.

Taken by surprise at Mr Kruger's knowledge of the house Dad joked:

"You didn't want to buy it also, did you?"

"Certainly not!" cried Mr Kruger.

"What do you mean by that tone?" asked Dad who was now looking a bit concerned.

"I've worked there before and I don't like the feel of the place. It's not normal," said Mr Kruger.

With a puzzled look upon his face Dad said, "Explain yourself?"

Mr Kruger leaned forward towards my dad and spoke in a hushed voice.

"There's been strange goings on in that

house. I've heard weird noises in it. Some of my equipment has gone missing too."

"Are you trying to tell me it's haunted?" laughed Dad.

Mr Kruger replied, "It's no laughing matter, I'll not work in that house for you. Goodnight!"

We looked at each other amazed at what we had just heard. Could the house really be haunted?

Dad reassured us, "He's as daft as a brush. I'll get someone else to do the work."

"Do you think he meant what he said?" asked Beth.

Mum replied, "There are no such things as ghosts – as we're going to find out. When we move in everything will be just fine."

"Yes, your mother's quite right. Don't let that wierdo electrician give you the creeps. He's probably too lazy to do the job," added Dad.

A few minutes later the plumber Dad had arranged to meet appeared. He was a small gentleman by the name of Mr Lennox. Mum showed him into the living room and sat him down in front of us all.

"Have you done much work out in Oddburgh, Mr Lennox?" began Dad.

Mr Lennox nodded and replied, "Yes, of course. There are a lot of rich pickings out that way."

"Oh good!" said Dad. "We've just bought a place out there and need some plumbing upgraded."

"That sounds fine. What's the name of the street?" inquired Mr Lennox.

Dad replied, "Blackday Avenue, number 13."

Mr Lennox smiled uneasily and said:

"You're not having me on here, are you Mr Todd?"

Dad looked perplexed by Mr Lennox's

question and said, "Of course I'm not. What's your problem?"

"It's not my problem: it's yours!" cried Mr Lennox.

Becoming more agitated Dad said, "Explain yourself?"

"That house has got a reputation Mr Todd. All the tradesmen I know won't set foot in the place. There have been too many rumours about it," said Mr Lennox.

"Rumours!" cried Dad. "You mean ghosts and things going bump in the night?"

"That's what they say," Mr Lennox replied.

"But that's superstitious nonsense!" cried Dad.

"That may be," said Mr Lennox. "But I'll not work in there!"

Dad threw his hands in the air.

"Well thanks for nothing Mr Lennox. I expected to strike a deal with a plumber but instead I listen to a coward about his fear of ghosts. Goodnight."

As Mr Lennox left our house he cried at Dad: "You'll have a hard job finding anyone to do any work in that house for you!"

Slamming the door shut Dad cried: "Superstitious fools! This is almost the end of the 20th century. How can anyone believe in ghosts?"

"It seems the tradesmen in this town do," said Mum.

"Don't let these guys worry you." Dad said, recognising our fears about the house. They probably just use the haunted house routine as a way to bump up their prices. I wouldn't be surprised if those two jokers called back later offering to do the job under protest, but for more money. That's the way it sometimes works kids."

I suppose Dad was right. Working in a haunted house would be a good excuse to

Chapter 5

inflate your price. But what if they weren't joking?

"So we're still moving then?" I asked Dad.

He clapped his hands together and beamed.

"Of course we are! It will be the best move we ever make. Wait and see!"

Chapter 6

The day of the move had arrived. Everything was packed and ready to go. How we had managed to squeeze so much stuff into our little house I'll never know. Maybe it was a good idea that we were finally moving to a bigger place.

Dad had chosen a removal firm from out of town. He had reasoned that any local removal company would try to hit us with the haunted house routine and bump up their price. They packed up the van quietly and efficiently and soon we were on our way without any fuss.

"On our way at last!" cried Dad to us in the car.

Mum held back a tear and said, "Wave bye-bye to the old house."

We all waved and for a moment thought about all the happy times we had spent there. But today was the big move and we had to prepare ourselves. We didn't want to live in the new place at all, and now was the time to spook Dad out of living there. What fun we had planned!

Even though it was a bright sunny day, Blackday Avenue was still starved of light. The gloom seemed to worsen as we approached number 13. The sight of our new home sent a shudder down my spine. I could see it was having the same effect on my brother and sisters. We'd forgotten how frightening and imposing the building looked.

"Everybody out!" cried Dad with a happy voice.

The removal men stood ready and waiting for Dad to open up the house. They seemed keen enough to get on with the job despite the reputation of the house.

As Dad was about to put the key in the door it slowly creaked open as if by itself. We all stared in trepidation as the dark hallway came into view. Maybe the place was haunted!

Then I caught sight of the strange figure of Davina Metz. She stood there, dressed all in black again.

"I thought I'd come to welcome you to your new home," she said.

"You gave us all a bit of a turn there," said my father, visibly relieved. "Maybe you should have let us know about your idea to welcome us? The kids are a bit funny about this house and seeing the door open like that won't have helped any."

Davina Metz's face registered no embarrassment, instead she smiled the most sickly, hideous smile I have ever seen..

"You have my apologies Mr Todd," she said, "but really, there's no reason to be afraid. There's no such thing as ghosts you know."

Gary whispered in my ear, "But you do a good impression of one!"

I had to stifle a giggle after Gary made that remark. Mum looked sternly at us to stop us causing any further embarrassment.

Miss Metz noted, "I see that you haven't had any work done on the house yet."

"No, we've had problems getting people to work here. There's a crazy story going around that the house is haunted," said Dad sheepishly.

"Well, there are plenty of candles around the house for you to use until you get the power back on," said Miss Metz.

"That shouldn't take long dear, should it?" remarked Mum towards Dad.

Dad instantly replied, "We'll have lights on in a jiffy!"

Miss Metz then departed saying, "I wish you all the best in your new house."

"Thank you for your help Miss Metz," said Dad as she left the house.

We all stood for a moment in the gloom of the darkened hallway. A second later I looked back out of the opened front door to see Davina Metz leaving down the driveway.

My eyes bulged when I noticed she was gone.

"Where did she go?" I cried.

The rest of my family turned to look outside as well. Davina Metz had, once again, mysteriously disappeared.

"OK, so she's gone," said Dad. "What's the big deal? We've got loads of work to do."

A few minutes later the removal men began bringing in our furniture, followed by what seemed hundreds of boxes. We all set to work unpacking.

After about an hour the removal van was unloaded. The men sat around for a minute and passed a bottle of lemonade to each other.

"Thirsty work?" said Dad.

One of the men replied, "Oh that was quite an easy load. No problems there."

Dad gave them each a tip and said, "Thank you very much for your help."

As they got up to leave one of the men appeared to be looking for something.

"Lost something?" inquired Mum.

The man replied, "I can't find my baseball cap. I could have sworn I put it down over there."

He was pointing to a packing case in the corner of the hallway.

"Maybe you left it in your van," reasoned Mum.

The man went out to his van and appeared a minute later.

"It's not in the van. I'm sure I left it in the corner over there."

Dad questioned us.

"Did any of you see this man's cap?"

We looked at each other and shook our heads. I was sure none of us had noticed the cap, let alone hidden it somewhere else.

"Are you sure about that kids?" said Mum.

Beth piped up, "We were all too busy to be bothered with a cap."

"Oh well," said the removal man. "Maybe I'm starting to lose my marbles."

Dad reassured him, "If we come across your baseball cap, we'll make sure you get it back."

The man left saying, "Can't say fairer than that."

When the removal van had departed Dad announced, "I'll need to see what I can do about the power in here. Now where's my torch?"

"It will be with the rest of the tools over there, where you left them," replied Mum.

After rummaging through the tool bag for a minute Dad cried, "Ok, who's moved the torch?"

"Not me," said Beth.

"Haven't seen it," replied Gary.

Karen slowly shook her head from side to side in response.

"Maybe you left it at the old house?" I answered.

"I made sure it was packed with all the other tools," said Mum.

Dad was getting angry and said, "Well, its not here now."

He then stomped off in the direction of the basement with his torch saying, "Luckily I've got an old spare one that should do the job."

I looked at Karen suspiciously. She had the idea to frighten Dad out of the house. Had she started to work on him already? I took her aside to ask her.

"Karen, have you started your tricks already?" I asked her.

Karen looked surprised and replied, "What have I been up to?"

"You've been hiding things, haven't you?" I said.

She replied, "I haven't been up to anything."

"Honest?" I quizzed her.

"Honest, Alex. Cross my heart and hope to die," replied Karen.

Maybe it was just coincidence that first the cap and now the torch had gone missing. I mean it couldn't be ghosts could it?

Chapter 7

As afternoon gave way to evening the house began to become quite dark inside. Mum and me went around lighting the candles that Miss Metz had left behind. Dad had been down in the basement for ages trying to put the power back on. It came as no surprise to us that he hadn't succeeded yet.

He would reappear from time to time saying, "It's a really old fuse box," or "I don't have the parts," or "I don't have the proper tools."

We had heard it all before though. Any

job that Dad tried to do around the house usually turned out like this. He would tinker around for hours and usually make a mess of the job he was supposed to be doing. The typical ending to one of Dad's repairs was to call out a proper tradesman to repair the damage that he had done. But there was no stopping Dad.

The good news was at least we had a gas supply and could cook. Mum prepared a simple meal that we ate in the kitchen by candlelight. Despite his failure to get the power back on, Dad was happy tonight.

"It's the simple things that make you appreciate life," said Dad with a peaceful smile on his face.

"With you as our repair man we have to accept the simple things!" Mum remarked jokingly.

"Soon be time for bed kids," said Dad.

Chapter 7

I winked at Karen as she smiled at me. We were about to try and scare the wits out of Dad.

"We'll go and explore the house a bit before we got to bed," I told Dad.

"OK, don't be too long though" Dad replied, "and stay out of the basement and the attic. It's too dark and you might fall and hurt yourselves."

"Don't worry Dad, well be careful," said Beth.

We ran upstairs to one of the bedrooms where we would be spending our first night.

"What shall we do then?" I asked the others.

Karen saw all the bedding in the room. "Let's all put these white sheets over our heads and jump out at Dad."

"Great idea!" cried Gary.

Giggling as we threw the sheets over our

heads, we heard Dad coming up the stairs. His footsteps came nearer and nearer as we hid from him in complete silence.

Then I whispered to the others, "On the count of three. One . . . two . . . three!"

We leaped out at him shouting in ghostly voices, "Woooahhhh!"

Nothing happened. He only stared blankly at us.

Again we flapped the sheets around our heads and shouted, "Woooahhhh!"

"Is that the best you can do?" commented Dad.

Pulling the sheets off our heads we felt really stupid. Dad hadn't been frightened in the slightest. It was almost as if he was expecting us to pull a stunt like that.

Beth tried to explain, "We just thought we'd play a joke on you."

It had been a long day and Dad was tired, but at least he kept his sense of humour.

Chapter 7

"You couldn't frighten the skin off a rice pudding!" cried Dad.

As he left us to get on with another chore, Gary whispered to me, "Just you wait and see."

Back in the bedroom we put the sheets back where we had found them. We had to come up with another idea and quickly.

"I know," said Beth, "when Dad goes down stairs let's bang on the pipes and make ghostly moans."

Karen smiled naughtily.

"Yes, let's get some newspapers and roll them up into tubes. Then our voices will sound more deep and frightening," she said, giving a delighted laugh.

As Dad descended the stairs we sneaked into the bathroom. It was full of old pipes just waiting to be tapped. The sound would easily carry downstairs to the bathroom and kitchen.

"What can we tap the pipe with?" asked Gary.

I looked around, but there was nothing solid that could give the pipes a good bash. Karen then disappeared out of the bathroom. A moment later she reappeared holding a metal wall bracket.

"Where did you find that?" I asked her?

She answered, "It was in the bedroom on the floor."

"You think of everything, don't you!" said Beth.

Karen replied feeling pleased with herself, "Of course."

I began to tap lightly on the pipes as the others faintly moaned into the newspaper tubes, "Woooahhhh! Woooahhhh! Woooahhhh!"

There was no response from downstairs.

"Make it louder," said Gary.

I wrapped on the pipes a lot harder and

the others began shouting into the newspaper tubes. We stopped for a few seconds and listened for any response downstairs.

"Are they deaf?" whispered Beth.

I replied, "Let's try one more time."

As we went about our naughty business suddenly we got the shock of our lives.

"Boo!" cried a voice out of the gloom.

We jumped out of our skins with fright. It was Dad. While we were busy making a noise he must have sneaked up the stairs.

"You'll really have to do better than that," said Dad.

Gary said, "What do you mean by frightening the life out of us like that?"

"So it's OK for you to try and frighten me, but I'm not allowed to try and frighten you back?" Dad replied.

"That's not fair, you're an adult," said Karen.

Dad stuck out his tongue at Karen and

wiggled his backside. He was as big a kid as the rest of us. His antics had not amused Karen though, and she stood there with arms folded and a petted lip.

"Now, you lot – no more jokes. Behave and get washed and go to your beds. I'm trying to get the lights on before the night is out, so don't disturb me any more!" Dad warned us.

We didn't feel like sleeping just yet, so we went back to one of the bedrooms and discussed our plight. It didn't seem as though we would be able to frighten Dad into changing his mind about the house. He seemed to see right through our feeble attempts to frighten him.

Beth said, "What can we do now? Dad seems to know what we're up to and isn't impressed at all."

"Yes, maybe we'd better leave things until the morning and had longer to think on how we can change Dad's thoughts about the house," I said.

"But he doesn't seem frightened of anything."Karen stated.

"Oh, we'll think of something," I said.

Then a moment later, Dad's footsteps came rushing up the stairs and along the landing towards us. He came into the bedroom and from his expression he was not amused.

"What did I just say?" he cried.

We looked at each other in puzzlement as his question. Was it one of terrible jokes again.

"I thought I told you to stop annoying me while I'm trying to fix the electricity," Dad continued.

I couldn't understand what he meant and said, "What do you mean, Dad. We've been up here all along."

"Is that so?" said Dad. "Well how come

I've been hearing lots of strange noises downstairs?"

Beth asked, "What sort of noises?"

"You should know. It must have been you lot who were making them," barked Dad.

As I looked at my brother and sisters we gave each other a shrug of the shoulders to indicate that we hadn't a clue what Dad was on about. It no longer seemed like one of his jokes. He was being serious.

I spoke up for us and said, "We haven't done anything Dad. Honest!"

"Well I've been hearing weird noises downstairs and it wasn't your Mum that was making them," said Dad.

"It wasn't us Dad. We've been in this room since you last spoke to us," Karen said.

"That's true, Dad. Tell us what sort of noises you heard?" asked Gary.

Dad seemed to believe us at last and said, "They were sort of grinding and chopping noises. It was as if someone was preparing meat or cooking."

"That's weird!" stated Beth. "You must be hearing things. Maybe this house is getting to you Dad?"

Dad said, "Well I'm sure I heard noises. Maybe there's a simple explanation – such as: you lot were responsible."

I said again, "Honest, Dad it wasn't us."

Dad turned to go back downstairs and said, "It's late. Get washed and get to bed. No excuses."

In unison we said, "Yes."

Was it possible that something, other than us, had been spooking Dad? I didn't like to dwell on that thought for too long as a chill ran down my spine.

Chapter 8

The bathroom was in darkness as we stood outside it. I don't think any of us liked the thought of spending time in there alone, so we decided to all go in and wash together. Between us we only had one candle. We entered the bathroom and I placed the candle on a ledge next to the basin where we would wash and brush our teeth.

Gary was just about to turn the taps on when a sudden icy breeze wafted through the bathroom. The flame flickered for a while in the breeze and then went out. Apart from the very faint candlelight coming from the landing we were in darkness. It felt uneasy in here and the hairs on the back of my neck began to rise.

"The window must be open," explained Beth.

I was certain it was closed before and replied, "I'm sure it was shut when we arrived this afternoon and had our first look around."

"Well somebody must have opened it then, silly!" cried Beth.

I felt very uneasy about this room and said, "Let's just wash quickly and get to bed."

"Yes, let's get out of here quickly it's scary," said Karen.

The taps were very stiff through lack of use and Gary had trouble opening them. After some straining with them, Gary prised them open and the pipes began to rattle with the air trapped in them. Then after a few more seconds we heard the rush of water gushing into the basin.

It was so dark in the bathroom that Gary had to feel around the basin to locate the plug and the plughole. Eventually he managed to match them together and the sound of water running down the plughole ceased.

Gary said, "This water feels funny."

"What do you mean funny?" I asked.

Gary replied, "It doesn't feel like water. It's feels sort of thick."

"Come on Gary, just get washed and let us have our turn so as we can get out of here quickly," said an agitated Beth.

I reasoned, "Maybe the water is just dirty and full of silt."

"It would help if we could see the water properly," said Gary.

"Well, at the moment we can't, so get a move on!" cried Beth.

I put my hands in the water and it immediately felt strange. It was sort of thick and slippery. I reasoned that the water must be absolutely filthy. Was it full of slime or something?

"That doesn't feel like clean water at all," I stated.

We jumped out of our skins as Dad shouted from downstairs, "I've done it! I'm about to put the lights on kids."

A few seconds later the house lit up with bright light. We were very relieved that the darkness had been lifted. Every light in the house must have been left switched on as suddenly the house was filled with light. It was a mystery to me that a fuse didn't blow with the sudden surge of power. For a moment we screwed up our eyes and were blinded by the intensity of the light that was now in the bathroom.

Then, a few seconds later, as our eyes

adjusted again to the light we screamed with horror. I couldn't believe what I was seeing.

"Ahhhhh! It's blood!"

There on my hands was dark red blood. Blood also dripped from Gary's hands and his face. In the basin was a pool of thick red blood. There was blood everywhere! Blood had come out of the taps!

"Dad! Mum! Help!" we all cried.

A ghostly, deep and horrible voice from out of nowhere then said:

"Who wants a blood bath?"

This was followed by the most cruel and evil laughter that I've ever heard. It frightened me to my very core.

"Let's get out of here!" screamed Beth.

As we lunged for the door it slammed shut with terrific force. I grabbed it and tried to turn the handle but it wouldn't budge. It was as if some evil invisible force was preventing me from opening the door.

The ghostly voice repeated:
"Who wants a blood bath?"

Gary's hands clasped over mine as we frantically tried to open the bathroom door to escape. The handle wouldn't budge no matter how hard we tried.

Karen cried, "Help Dad! Please help – quickly!"

Dad's voice sounded close by as he said, "This had better not be one of your tricks again. My sense of humour is wearing rather thin."

"We can't get the door open!" I screamed.

Quite suddenly the handle turned and the door opened. There stood Dad with a grim face.

"It's blood Dad!" cried Gary holding up his blood drenched hands. "It came out of the taps."

Dad looked not amused and said, "Don't be so stupid. Let me see."

He looked at our hands and then into the basin full of blood. For a second he looked confused as the colour began to drain from his face. He began to look very pale and ill.

Dad was beginning to sway as he said, "You're right. It's blood!"

With those words his eyes closed and he feinted to the floor with an almighty thud.

"Mum! Mum! Come quickly!" shouted Beth.

In a flash Mum was racing up the stairs to where Dad lay.

"What's happened?" she cried as she felt for Dad's pulse. "Why have you got blood on your hands? Did you cut yourself?"

I was shaking as I explained, "Dad fainted when he realised it was blood. It came out of the taps."

"Blood on tap?" said Mum with a tone of disbelief.

The lights then began to flicker and fade.

"What on earth is going on?" cried Mum.

The power went off again as the ghostly voice repeated:

"Who wants a blood bath?"

Karen screamed and shouted:

"Look! On the stairs."

We gasped in terror as we looked towards the stairs. In a strange eerie light we saw a headless figure dressed in a bloody butcher's apron. It was holding a huge knife dripping with blood. We winced as it began to come towards us.

"Run for it!" screamed Mum at us.

We raced along the landing and into a bedroom. Mum was last in and locked the door behind her. We held each other tightly in the dim candlelight praying for our lives.

The footsteps of the headless figure came slowly along the landing towards us. With a thud, the door received a massive blow.

The point of the bloody butcher's knife protruded through the door.

"Ha ha! Who wants a blood bath then my little friends?" cried the headless figure from the other side of the door.

"What do you want with us?" cried Beth.

The evil voice replied?

"I want all the blood that runs in your veins!"

A long ghostly laugh then rang in our ears for what seemed ages, only to be broken by the lights coming back on. Maybe Dad had woken up and put the power on again?

"Hey! The power is back on," cried Gary. "Maybe Dad or somebody has come to save us?"

Mum went to the door and listened for a while. She beckoned me over to put my ear to the door as well. I couldn't hear a thing.

"Sounds quiet out there now kids," said

Mum. "We'll have to see if your Dad is alright."

Karen sobbed as she said, "I don't want to do out there. The horrible headless figure will get us all."

Mum reassured her and said, "I think the ghost has gone now. It'll be OK Karen. I promise we'll all stick together."

"But you said there were no such things as ghosts!" cried Karen.

With trembling hands Mum slowly eased the door open and peered through the small gap.

"The coast is clear Kids. Let's go!" she whispered.

One by one we crept nervously out onto the landing. At any moment I was expecting to be attacked by the headless figure. What did it want with us?

"He's gone!" cried Mum.

Dad was no longer lying where he had

Chapter 8

fainted. He was nowhere to be seen. Could he have chased the headless figure away and put the power back on? I hoped with my life that this was so.

Chapter 9

Beth said, "Where has he gone?"

"Maybe he's gone to try and find us?" replied Mum.

"He could have lost his bearings after fainting and is looking for us somewhere else in the house," I said. "Maybe he's outside looking for us?"

Gary then said what none of us wanted to hear: "The ghost must have got him."

"Oh no! Poor Daddy!" sobbed Karen.

"He'll be alright," I said, putting my arm around my little sister. "Just you wait and see."

Mum said, "Let's try to find him."

The split-second after she spoke the lights began to dim and flicker again. Once again we were standing in almost total darkness. The hairs on my neck began to stand up even more than they had before.

"On no! Not again!" screamed Beth pointing towards the stairs.

There, once again, on the stairs was the bloody headless figure. It was edging, step by step, towards us with its deadly weapon. We instantly turned to make towards the bedroom and safety once more. To our utter horror another ghoul was standing at the bedroom door.

"We're trapped!" cried Gary.

The other ghoul had only one arm and a horribly scarred pale face. It gave us a horrible grin, exposing black rotting teeth as it edged towards us. In its only hand it held a bloody meat cleaver.

Chapter 9

It's deep evil voice exclaimed:

"I'm going to make mince out of you!"

Terrified, we were rooted to the spot as we watched one of the ghosts, then the other, edge closer and closer to us. How could we escape such a horrible death?

"What will we do Mum?" cried Beth.

Mum said, "Hold on to me tight."

Embracing each other as though it was to be our last few seconds, Karen suddenly screamed, "Quick into the attic!"

We'd been so petrified that the ladders to the attic had escaped our notice. Mum jumped in a flash and pulled the ladders down. The ghosts were almost upon us as I raced up the ladders and tried to open the attic hatch. I pushed and pushed but the hatch wouldn't budge.

"It won't budge!" I screamed.

Gary came up the ladders and we both pushed. With a final supreme effort the hatch flew open and we dived up into the attic. Quickly we pulled up Karen and then Beth. Mum was the last on the ladders and the ghosts were reaching out and almost touching her. They were within an inch of grabbing Mum when we grasped her hands and pulled her into the attic. We slammed the attic door on the ghosts and sat upon it.

Breathing a sigh of relief we thought the worst was over for the moment. Then the hatch was pushed from underneath.

"They're trying to break in!" I cried.

Mum ordered, "Quick everybody! Sit on the hatch."

There was push after push from underneath. Could we keep the blood-thirsty ghosts as bay?

One of the ghosts said:

"We'll have you for butcher meat!"

The sound of evil laughter rang in our ears, but we were able to keep the ghosts from opening the hatch. After a short while their attempts to gain entry to the attic ceased. Not a sound could be heard in the house down below.

At first the attic seemed quite dark. It had a huge skylight though, and after a while the moonlight streaming through it enabled us to see around the attic without too much trouble.

Looking around the contents of the attic I noticed two familiar objects on a table.

"Look, Dad's torch is on that table over there," I said.

"And that man's cap too," Beth added.

Gary asked, "How did they get up here?"

"I don't know," I replied, "but when we tried to open the hatch it felt as though it hadn't been tried in ages."

"It must have been the ghosts!" exclaimed Karen.

Beth asked, "What will we do now?"

"I don't know," replied Mum.

Karen sobbed and said, "I wish Dad was here."

"We all wish that, Karen, but he'll be alright," said Mum.

It seemed stupid for all of us to remain sitting on the hatch so I said, "Let's move that chest onto the hatch. It looks heavy enough to keep them out."

Gary and me shoved the chest next to the hatch as Mum and the girls remained sitting on it. Then, in one swift movement, we pushed the heavy chest onto the hatch as Mum and the girls leapt off it.

"That should be safe for now," said Mum.

The attic was brimming with junk. In the moonlight I began to examine the contents and found a huge sign. It read:

"SLAUGHTER & SONS
BUTCHERS
ODDBURGH."

"Look at this?" I said.

Mum explained, "Maybe they're the people who last owned the house."

Next to the sign I came across a pile of papers. They were marked in red ink, "Final Demand."

Alongside the pile was a box full of letters from a Solicitor's office. I picked up Dad's torch, switched it on, and began to read them.

"What does bankruptcy mean, Mum?" I asked.

Mum sighed and looked angry.

"What are you asking me that for at a time like this?"

"It's what all these letters are about," I replied.

"It's when a business hasn't got enough money to keep itself going and pay the people it owes money to." Mum said.

"That bankruptcy thing must have happened to Slaughter & Sons then," I said. "Maybe it's got something to do with the ghosts."

Beth said, "Could be, but how's that going to help us at this precise moment?"

"Come here kids," said Mum. "Each of you spread out in the attic and put your ears to the floor and listen for noises."

Obeying her wish we all went to different parts of the attic and got down on our hands and knees. I listened for a while but couldn't hear a sound.

"Did anyone hear anything?" whispered Mum.

We all shook our heads. The house down below was silent.

Mum said, "We can't stay up here forever. We'll have to go and look for Dad, OK. It sounds as if the ghosts have gone."

Trying to be as quiet as possible we eased the heavy chest off the attic door. I got on my hands and knees and lifted the hatch by a tiny amount. In the dim candlelight the landing seemed to clear of any lurking ghosts.

"It looks clear to me," I told Mum.

Mum said, "Quickly kids, down with the ladders. Gary, don't forget the torch."

I pulled the hatch open and holding my breath with fear I stepped onto the ladder. My heart was pounding as I reached the bottom. In a moment the rest of my family joined me.

Mum whispered, "Stay alert kids. We're going downstairs to look for Dad."

Chapter 10

As quietly as possible we tiptoed along the landing and onto the staircase. Mum had taken the torch and was shining it ahead of us to look for danger. About half way down the stairs the lights suddenly flickered into life again.

"Maybe Dad has put the power back on?" said Beth.

Feeling a little less frightened we reached the bottom of the stairs. Dad was nowhere to be seen. I suppose that meant we would have to search through every room for him.

"I'll check if Dad's in the basement first," pronounced Mum.

She uneasily opened the door to the basement with us at her back. I could see that the basement was in darkness.

Mum whispered, "Are you down there, Bill?"

There was no reply.

She asked gain with a slightly raised voice, "Bill! Are you down there."

Still there was no reply. If he wasn't down there, then where was he? We went over to a door that opened into one of the living rooms. It was in darkness but I switched the light on straight away. The room was empty. Door by door we went around all the rooms on the ground floor. There was not a trace of Dad to be found.

"We're not leaving this house until we find him," stated Mum.

There was one last door to try. This door

Chapter 10

entered onto the downstairs bathroom. With great hopes of finding Dad on the other side I turned the handle and gently pushed the door open. That very instant the lights flickered and faded out again.

"Oh, Oh!" I cried.

My body froze as I fully opened the door. I couldn't even utter a word to my family. There, in the bathroom, stood two horrible looking figures. One was a female in a dress covered with blood. Her hands and head were covered in blood also. Beside her stood a younger figure covered in blood as well.

The figures turned their horrible evil faces to look at me and said together:

"Who wants a blood bath?"

Beth screamed, "Run for it!"

Where would we run? At first we made for the front door. Gary pulled the door open and to his horror the headless figure stood there flashing the butcher's knife. We turned and fled towards the stairs.

"Oh no!" cried Karen.

At the top of the stairs was the figure with only one arm. The meat cleaver was raised above its head as if ready to strike us at any moment. What would we do? Our state of panic was not allowing us to think straight.

Then Karen provided the answer. Her little voice yelled, "Quick, into the basement!"

In a flash we were all through the basement door and on the steps. Mum slammed the door, behind us, and threw her weight against it. Luckily Gary still had the torch which he immediately switched on. I spied a chair at the bottom of the steps and rushed down to get it.

The ghosts were banging on the door. I grabbed the chair and ran up to where Mum was. Together we wedged the chair between the door handle and the top step to prevent them getting in.

"Phew! That was close," I said.

On the other side of the door the ghosts were screaming:

"Who wants a blood bath?! Who wants a blood bath?!"

After a while they became silent again. We all breathed a sigh of relief that they appeared to have disappeared again. Then I thought I heard a noise. It was very faint, but I was sure I heard something.

"Shh!" I pleaded.

The noise grew louder and louder. It was a grating sort of noise; the sound of metal grinding against metal. The noise grew louder still until it was ringing in my ears. Then in horror I realised what the noise was.

I cried, "Mum, that's the sound of them sharpening their knives!"

All the ghosts then let out cackles of evil laughter and one of them said:

"We shall make some nice fillets out of your young bodies!"

"Let's see if we can get out of here and into the garden," said Gary.

Mum frowned at him and said, "I told you we're not leaving this house without your Dad."

I added, "But maybe he's outside wondering around in a daze."

"OK, maybe you're right," said Mum.

Gary tried the door that opened onto the garden. It wouldn't budge.

"It must be locked," said Gary. "And there's no sign of a key."

Beth said, "So, we're stuck in this dingy basement until the ghosts go away!"

"Or they get us," said Karen.

Mum snapped at Karen.

"Don't think that way. Of course we're

going to escape. And your Dad will be alright too!"

Suddenly the noise of sharpening knives stopped. The sound of evil laughter was gone too. I went up to the basement door and listened.

"Seems all clear out there now," I whispered.

Mum said, "Let's make a run for it then. Kids, no messing around, just straight out the front door."

I pulled the chair from under the door handle and threw the door open. In a second I had rushed through the hallway and had grabbed the front door handle. I didn't even look around to see if the ghosts were still there. I turned the handle and opened the door.

Instantly I cried, "Help!'

There in the doorway stood a tall thin figure wearing a hood over his head. It must be another ghost! The figure raised its hands to the hood and removed it to reveal the grey hair of an old man.

"I'm sorry did I frighten you?" he said.

Chapter 11

We all stared at the old grey figure for a moment. On looking at him further he didn't seem like the other ghosts.

Beth said, "You're not a ghost are you?"

"On no! Whatever gave you that idea?" said the old man.

Mum confessed, "I'm sorry but you wouldn't believe what we've been through."

The old man said, "I'm Alfred Hale from across the street. I saw the lights flashing on and off and thought there may be something wrong. Can I be of any help? You all look as if you've seen a ghost!"

"We have!" I cried. "Several of them."

Mr Hale came into the hall and explained.

"Well, they do say this place is haunted. I've never seen any ghosts myself, but that's what they say."

"Go on," urged Mum.

"There was a family that lived here called the Slaughters," he explained. "They had a butcher's business in town but they ran into difficulties."

"That explains all the stuff in the attic," I interrupted.

He continued.

"One night they invited over all the people they owed money to. They said they wanted to work out repayments with them or something like that. Anyway, once they had them all inside the house they locked the doors. They must have been completely insane."

He paused at this point and looked at my

Mum as if he didn't want to tell the rest of the story in front of us kids.

"Please tell us the rest," insisted Mum. "These kids have been through a lot tonight."

"Very well," said Mr Hale. "When the doors were locked the whole Slaughter family pulled out their knives and cleavers and chopped their guests to death. They hid the bodies in the water tank. A few days later, when the police arrived to investigate, they say that the taps ran red with blood."

"That explains a lot," said Mum.

Mr Hale went on, "When the police tried to arrest them the family turned against each other. They grabbed their butchery tools and set about each other. Before they police could do anything the father's head was chopped off and the eldest son's arm was hacked off too."

"Was there a wife and a younger son?" asked Beth.

"Yes they died through loss of blood along with the eldest son whose arm was chopped off," replied Mr Hale.

Mum said, "What a horrible tale. No wonder this place is haunted."

"Yes, it's quite gruesome isn't it? The house was deserted for years until your family came along and bought it," said Mr Hale.

"Well thank goodness you are here Mr Hale. You haven't seen my husband outside in the grounds have you?" inquired Mum.

Mr Hale replied, "No, it's very quiet out there."

"He must still be in the house then," cried Karen.

I added, "Yes, we must find him and get out of here!"

Immediately after uttering those words a freezing wind shot through the hallway making us all shiver. The front door crashed shut with tremendous force making the whole house shake.

Gary grabbed the front door handle but the door refused to open. Mr Hale then added his strength to try and open the door.

"It's completely jammed," he said.

In an instant the ghosts had reappeared. They stood ready with their knives and cleavers.

"Oh my word!" cried Mr Hale.

The ghosts cackled:

"Who wants a blood bath?!"

We stood in a tight bunch in the centre of the hallway. The ghosts circled around us waving their shiny metal implements and laughing in a horrible evil fashion. Who could save us now?

Out of the corner of my eye I saw a fifth ghost approaching from the kitchen. It was all ghostly white and wearing a butchers apron, but also a cap. It attracted the attention of the female ghost and beckoned her to towards him. The female ghost slowly edged towards the fifth ghost.

The fifth ghost said:

"I am the Master Butcher. I am not afraid of you. Return to the hell that you came from."

For some strange reason amidst all the fear and mayhem the voice of the ghostsounded strangely familiar. Was my mind playing tricks on me?

In a flash there was a terrible wail from the female ghost and she faded away without a trace. What on earth was going on, I wondered?

Seeing a gap between the ghosts Gary shouted:

"Quick! To the stairs."

We raced up the stairs and onto the landing. The ghosts lurched up the stairs behind us.

Chapter 11

The younger ghost turned to face the new ghost, who was following behind, and cried:

"I'm going to make sausages out of you!"

"You couldn't make sausages if you tried. That's why you went out of business!" said the newcomer. "Now be gone you foul creature. The Master Butcher has no fear of the likes of you. Be gone!"

With a terrible howl the small ghost faded away. Now there were only three ghosts to deal with. The headless figure and the one armed figure edged closer and closer to us, with the new ghost just behind them.

"The attic or the bedroom?" said Beth.

I raced up the ladder and tried to open the hatch to the attic. It wouldn't move at all. Mum and Mr Hale frantically tried to force it open but it wouldn't budge.

The ghosts were almost upon us as I shouted, "Run for it! To the bedroom."

By this time I saw that the one armed

ghost had been attracted to the strange new ghost. It turned and began edging its way towards the newcomer waving the meat cleaver.

"Why do you come among us?" said the one armed ghost. "I'll have a bath in your blood!"

The new ghost stood there and cried: "You can't frighten me. I'm the Master Butcher. If anyone's going to do some butchery around here it's going to be me! Return to the evil place from where you came!"

There was a sickening cry as the one armed ghost vanished from our sight.

"What's going on?" said Mum. "It's as if that new ghost is trying to save us."

All of us gathered in the bedroom as the headless ghost grew nearer and nearer. It was waving its knife about in a frenzied motion now.

"I'll kill you all!" yelled the headless figure.

We slammed the door shut and locked it. The ghosts could fight it out amongst themselves.

"How dare you interfere!" cried the headless ghost to the newcomer.

"You're not fit to be a butcher!" replied the new ghost.

The door shook as the knife plunged into the door again and again. The wood was starting to splinter. I was sure the door couldn't hold for much longer.

"I wish I'd never came to help you," said Mr Hale.

Karen replied, "Thanks all the same, Mr Hale."

The new ghost cried, "You failed as a butcher. That is why your business failed. You are not good enough to bear the title of a butcher."

"It wasn't my fault!" cried the headless figure.

"You are nothing!" said the new ghost. "I have no fear of you. I'm the Master Butcher. What I say, goes!"

There was a horrible scream and the headless figure cried, "Nooooo!"

Then there was silence! What would we do now? Should we stay put and wait for dawn. It had been a long night and I looked at my watch. It was almost half past five. Dawn would be any minute now. Would the morning light save us from the ghost on the other side of the door?

Chapter 12

The ghost knocked on the door and said: "Its alright, you can come out now."

My mind must have playing tricks on me. It sounded exactly like Dad's voice. We looked at each other for a moment in puzzlement. Could the ghost really be Dad?

"It really sounds like your Dad's voice, doesn't it?" Mum said.

We nodded our heads in agreement, but Gary cautioned us.

"Maybe it's an evil trick to get us to open the door. Maybe the ghost will burst in and butcher us all!"

"You could be right," said Beth.

"Come on you lot, open the door! It's safe now," the ghost cried.

I glanced out of the bedroom window and noticed that the first light of dawn was appearing over the horizon. The coming of daylight should save us from the ghost.

"Look!" I said. "It's dawn and we should be alright now."

The voice from the other side of the door said:

"It's really me. I'm your Dad. I scared all those horrible ghosts away."

"Open the door," ordered Mum.

Mr Hale didn't seem so sure.

"Are you certain about what you're about to do?"

"I think so," replied Mum.

With a sense of doubt I slowly turned the key in lock and opened the door.

"Ahhh!" I screamed as the door opened onto the landing.

Chapter 12

There, before us, stood the pale white ghost in the butcher's apron and cap. It had all been a ghostly trick to get us to open the door!

"Boo!" it cried. "See, it's only me!"

In an instant my fears turned to unbridled joy. It was Dad. I could recognise his features.

He hugged me, and I hugged him back with all my might.

"You're not a ghost Dad, are you?" I asked.

He laughed and said, "Of course I'm not."

Then I noticed that I was covered in a pale white substance that must have rubbed off from Dad.

"What's this?" I asked.

"Flour!" he cried.

"But it makes you look like a ghost!" Mum cried.

Dad said, "I know. Rather convincing, isn't it?"

"Those other ghosts were certainly convinced anyway," commented Beth.

We all gathered around Dad and gave him a big hug. Mr Hale stood in the bedroom with a puzzled smile on his face.

"Would you mind telling me exactly what is going on around here?"he said.

"You've seen the ghosts around here?" Dad asked.

"Yes of course. They had me absolutely petrified. I thought I was going to end up as mincemeat," said Mr Hale.

Dad continued, "I thought the kids were just mucking around when they mentioned blood. I've always been a bit squeamish when it comes to blood and at the sight of it on my kids faces I fainted."

"We know," said Karen. "But where did you get to?"

Dad said, "I woke up feeling dazed and confused. You lot weren't around when I stumbled down the stairs trying to find you. While I was downstairs the ghosts of the woman and boy came after me. So I ran away and locked myself in the larder next to the kitchen."

"So how did you get covered in flour?" Gary asked.

Dad explained, "I must have been stumbling about in the darkness in the larder and knocked a jar of flour onto my head. It made me look quite ghostly, didn't it?"

"You had us convinced!" stated Mum.

"In the larder I also found this old butcher's apron and cap. In order to save us I thought I'd try and beat those ghosts at their own game. I decided I was the Master Butcher and I would tell them what to do," said Dad. "I would scare them all away!"

Beth said, "Gosh! You're so brave Dad."

Dad's chest seemed to swell at Beth's

comment, but it quickly deflated as Mum said:

"That's not at all like you is it?"

"I have my moments," said Dad.

"How did you think you could frighten the ghosts into leaving us Dad?" Karen asked.

"I don't know, Karen. I had to try something to save us all. It seemed like a good idea to fight them using the idea that they had failed as butchers. It worked too!" explained Dad.

Mr Hale added, "That was a great idea. You played on the fears of the ghosts that they were failures. You showed no fear of them and told them exactly what they were."

"That's about the size of it. I stood up to their ghostly antics and told them to leave," said Dad.

I couldn't believe it was that simple and

cried, "Was that all there was to it? We were frightened out of our wits!"

"Well someone had to do something," said Dad.

Mr Hale praised Dad:

"We're very glad that you did."

"I'm famished," said Dad. "Anyone for breakfast?"

"As long as it's over at my house. I've had enough shocks in this house to last me a lifetime," Mr Hale replied.

We gathered a few things together and went across the road to Mr Hale's house. Looking back towards the house, as we went down the driveway, it still had an evil gloomy look about it. What did Dad ever see in such an awful house?

Dad, himself, turned to take a long look at the house. He began to shake his head.

"Maybe you were right kids. That house isn't very welcoming, is it?" said Dad.

"I'm glad you agree at last," cried Karen.

Mum said, "We'll call the Estate Agents straight away and put it on the market."

What a relief! I don't think any of us could have spent another night in that evil place.

Mr Hale showed us into his house and sat us down in his large kitchen. He went to his fridge and brought out lots of things for breakfast.

"What would everybody like then? A full breakfast? Bacon, sausage, black pudding?" said Mr Hale.

We looked at one another around the breakfast table. I'm sure only one thought was in our minds. Butchers! My stomach turned at the very thought. Did Mr Hale have no feelings at all?

"I'll just have tea and toast," I said.

The rest of my family must have felt the same way and they too requested only tea and toast.

That was everyone apart from my Dad. Nothing could deter him from a good breakfast.

He rubbed his belly and said:

"I'll have the works, please. Did you buy them from a good butcher then?"

All together we cried:

"Dad, honestly!"

"What's your problem?" he replied.

That was typical Dad though. He simply didn't think like the rest of us. That's why we all loved him.

What a man!

We hope you enjoyed this story from the pen of
Edgar J. Hyde. Here are some other titles in the
Creepers series for you to collect:

The Ghostly Soldier
Doctor Death
Happy Halloween
Soul Harvest
Edgar Escapes!

This series was conceived by Edgar J Hyde and
much of the text was provided by his minions under slavish conditions and pain of death! Thank-
fully none of the minions defied their master and
so we can say 'thank you' to them for toughing it
out and making this series possible